My Two Uncles

J u d i t h   V i g n a

Albert Whitman & Company, Morton Grove, Illinois

B

Other Books by Judith Vigna

Black Like Kyra, White Like Me
Boot Weather
Grandma Without Me
I Wish Daddy Didn't Drink So Much
Mommy and Me by Ourselves Again
My Big Sister Takes Drugs
Nobody Wants a Nuclear War
Saying Goodbye to Daddy
She's Not My Real Mother
Uncle Alfredo's Zoo
When Eric's Mom Fought Cancer

The text of this book is set in Italia Book.
The illustrations are rendered in watercolor.
Design by Lucy Smith.

Library of Congress Cataloging-in-Publication Data
Vigna, Judith.
My two uncles / written and illustrated by Judith Vigna.
p. cm.
Summary: Elly's grandfather has trouble
accepting the fact that his son is gay.
ISBN 0-8075-5507-X
[1. Homosexuality—Fiction. 2. Uncles—Fiction.
3. Grandfathers—Fiction. 4. [E]] I. Title.
PZ7.V67Myt 1995   94-22007
                                          CIP
                                          AC

For E.K.
and her adored grandson C.T.
J.V.

I have two favorite uncles.
Uncle Ned is Daddy's brother. He's my real uncle. Uncle Phil is his friend.
I love it when Daddy takes me to their apartment.

There's a room where we paint and make things. Once when Daddy and I came for lunch, we made a wire mobile with foam bats and ghosts and flying witches. We got the idea from a Halloween show my uncles took me to.

This summer Uncle Ned and I made a diorama for my grandparents' golden wedding anniversary. They've been married fifty whole years. Mom and Daddy and I live with them.

To make the diorama, we built a stage and decorated it with gold ribbon streamers and a gold paper wedding cake. We got a copy of Gran and Grampy's old wedding picture, made a cutout of the figures, and glued it to cardboard. There were glittery gold curtains with a cord to pull them apart. We made it in my uncles' apartment because it was going to be a surprise. Uncle Phil helped us.

"I can't wait to see Gran and Grampy's faces when we bring it to the party!" I said.

The whole family was invited. So many relatives wanted to come that we were renting a huge tent to go in our yard.

The day before the anniversary lunch, I helped with the place cards.

"Can I sit between Uncle Ned and Uncle Phil?" I asked Daddy.

Suddenly Grampy jumped up from his chair. "You didn't invite Ned's friend, I hope," he said to Daddy. "You know he's not welcome in my house."

"What's Uncle Phil done?" I asked.

Gran shushed me and told me to play outside. I went out to the porch, but I could hear my father and Grampy arguing.

"Phil has lived with Ned for five years now," Daddy said. "Someday you will have to meet him."

"Well, it won't be tomorrow!" Grampy told him.

Then I heard Daddy sigh. "Ned will be hurt, and Elly will be really disappointed," he said.

Daddy came outside looking angry. He was carrying a telephone. I think he was talking to Uncle Ned.

"Isn't Uncle Phil coming to the party?" I asked when Daddy switched off the phone.

"No," he said. "And now Ned's so upset he doesn't want to come, either. He says he's tired of always going to family parties alone."

"What about our diorama?" I whispered. Uncle Ned was supposed to bring it with him.

Daddy smiled. "Ned will get it here in time—he promised."

It still wasn't fair. "Cousin Rob is bringing his girlfriend, and Grandma Sue's fiancé is coming. Why won't Grampy let Uncle Ned bring Uncle Phil?"

"It's because they're gay," Daddy said.

I didn't know what gay meant, exactly. But Daddy explained.

"Sometimes a man loves another man in the way a married couple love each other," he said. "Women who love each other like that are called lesbians. It's the way they are, just as Mommy and I are the way we are."

"So why is Uncle Ned welcome, and not Uncle Phil?"

"Ned is Grampy's own son," Daddy said. "But some people feel funny about seeing gays with their partners— even when it's a great guy like Phil. And some just don't think it's right for two men or two women to be a couple. But I don't think it's wrong. I think it's wrong when people hurt gays and lesbians just because of who they happen to be."

"I don't want my uncles to get hurt!"

"Neither do I," said Daddy. "And there's another thing: Some people worry that gays will try to change them, to make *them* gay. But no one can make another person gay."

"I wish Grampy would understand," I said.

That afternoon some workers came to put up the tent. There was a lot of sawing and hammering.

Later, Mom and Daddy drove to the bakery to pick up the anniversary cake, and Gran and Grampy went out to the yard to make sure everything got done. Gran told me to stay inside so I wouldn't get under everyone's feet.

I watched from the window. At last the tent was up. It looked just like a tent at the circus, only smaller. The workers started carrying in tables and chairs.

Everything was ready except our diorama.

When it started to get dark and people were leaving, I thought I'd better call my uncle. I called and called, but nobody was home except the answering machine.

What if Uncle Ned was so angry he didn't want to bring the present? Was he mad at *me*, too?

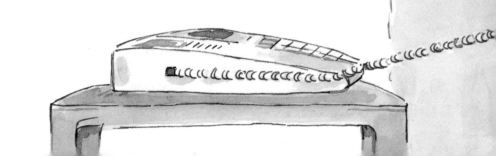

I didn't know what to think, so
I went out to the porch and waited.
Maybe Uncle Ned was on his way.

After awhile I heard a car
pull up by our gate. Uncle Ned
got out, carrying a big box.

Just then Grampy came out of the
tent. I got scared they'd fight, so I stayed
quiet. Uncle Ned handed him the box and
said, "Give this to Elly."

"You haven't changed your mind about coming
tomorrow?" asked Grampy.

"I'm sorry, Dad," my uncle told him. "Not without Phil."

As Uncle Ned walked away, I saw Grampy staring at Uncle
Phil, who was waiting in the car. I thought Grampy would get mad,
but he just stood there until Uncle Ned drove off.

I followed Grampy into the house. "Oh, there you are, Elly," he muttered. "Package for you." He dumped the box on the table.

When I opened the diorama in my room, it was even better than before. My uncle had hung a gold ring on the cord to make it easy to pull apart the curtains. And there was a tiny gold plaque with some fancy writing on it.

He'd written a note to me.

Dearest Elly,

Forgive me for not stopping to say hi, but it's hard for me to deal with Grampy right now. I love you and our family very much. But Phil is my family, too. Maybe one day Grampy will learn to love us for who we are, and then I hope we can all be together. I'll think of you tomorrow.

Your uncle Ned.

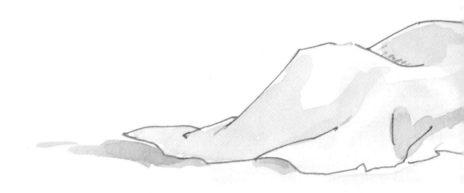

The next day was the party. It wasn't as much fun without my uncles, especially when the time came to show everyone the diorama. But when I opened the curtains, all the guests cheered.

"So *that* was the package Ned brought last night," Grampy said. "What a grand surprise!"

Gran put on her glasses. "Ned's written something under our names," she said, looking at the little gold plaque.

She read aloud: "'Happy anniversary to the golden couple from your granddaughter, Elly, and your loving son Ned.'"

Gran kissed me and Grampy. Then Grampy made a toast.

"To Elly," he said, raising his glass. "And to Ned, who chose not to be here today because of a stubborn old man, but who is loved by us all."

Some people clapped, and Mom and Daddy cried.

The next day after church, we stopped by to see Uncle Ned. Gran hugged him and Uncle Phil. "The diorama was the highlight of our party," she said. "I just had to come and thank you."

"Grampy says thank you, too," I said.

I took my two uncles to the window. They looked out where Grampy was waiting, and waved.

And Grampy waved back.